Thank you Caleb, Anna, Ethan, Bethany, and Madelyn. Always follow your dreams.

Lula and Todd Discover

The Secret Behind The Door

By Judy Pickrel

Illustrated by Charity Russell

CONTENTS

Chapter 1... 7

Chapter 2...11

Chapter 3...15

Chapter 4...19

Chapter 5...21

Chapter 6...27

Chapter 7...33

Chapter 8...39

Chapter 9...43

Chapter 10.......................................51

Chapter 11.......................................55

Chapter 12.......................................61

The King Loves You Too! 73

CHAPTER 1

JUST A MOUSE

If the need ever arose for someone to go on an epic adventure, no one would have thought about asking Lula. Why would they? Lula was a small ordinary mouse who was always hiding in her mouse hole. When she was with others, she was trying to not be noticed and blend into the wall. That is what makes the story of Lula being chosen for a dangerous rescue mission into the castle dungeon almost unbelievable.

Now like I said, Lula was small even for a mouse. When she was with others, she was never the center of attention. She was background for the main characters. Lula called a mouse named Long Tail a friend because she made sure to always be in the background when he told his tales. Long Tail always drew a crowd around himself as he told stories of how his tail almost cost him his life. Lula was horrified at the thought of losing any part of her cute little tail for a piece of cheese. Her tail was short already so there would be no flirting with the possibility

of losing any of HER tail. Her heart would pound at the maximum rate for a mouse of 632 beats a minute at the mere mention of any type of danger.

Cheddar was another mouse Lula considered to be her friend even though they never did anything together. Lula was at every talk Cheddar gave about cheese. He got his name because of his love for everything about cheese. Cheddar could command the attention of a room with his long list of the different cheeses available to those who were willing to face their fear. Mice were known to drool at his descriptions of the cheese flavors he had discovered. Lula did not consider herself an expert on anything. The thought of a group gathered around her and listening to her speak would almost cause her to faint. She was content being unnoticed. She was perfectly satisfied with the small crumbs of ordinary cheddar that she easily found lying along the edge of a room. She would never venture out into the middle of a room just for a larger chunk of cheese. Lula never even thought about going to unknown places in search of some exotic cheese that was too good for a little background mouse like her.

Then there was Belle. The most beautiful mouse ever born. Everyone wanted to be Belle's friend. Lula always made sure to be in the crowd around Belle. Belle was always happy and always having fun. Lula never thought of herself as beautiful and never the life of the party. Lula wished she could be free like Belle to live her life enjoying every moment with others crowded around. However, Lula never did anything without a very long detailed, step-by-step plan. To think of living her life moment by moment without being in full control was beyond terrifying.

Even though Lula lived with a large nest of mice, no one could have told you very much about her and some did not know she even existed. Let me say it again, Lula was just a plain ordinary mouse. She never did anything at the drop of a hat. She would have to stop and plan. Adventure was not something she was willing to take a risk to experience. To even think of leaving her safe little mouse hole for some wild adventure was just silly talk. She wanted to make sure she had thought of every possible danger and had a plan how to avoid it. But one day she made a mistake, or was it?

CHAPTER 2

LOST

As usual, Lula was up early before any of the other mice. It was still dark inside her little home and even darker outside her mouse hole where she would have to go to find a little crumb of cheddar. With her plan in her hand, she knew exactly the path she would take and the exact number of steps to find enough crumbs for the day. She had scurried down this path many times before and knew how much time she had before lights came on and others would be up and about.

She slipped out her mouse hole through the opening that was just big enough for her body to wiggle through, but not big enough for anything or anyone else to get in. That morning as she wiggled out through the small opening she was distracted by the sound of voices. Once again, her heart pounded at the maximum rate for a mouse of 632 beats a minute. She thought she might faint right then and there. Of course, Lula ran away from the voices. Nothing good could come from being curious.

When Lula was far enough away that the voices had faded, she stopped to catch her breath and get on with her day. She was way off schedule and soon everyone would be up. She looked around and nothing was familiar. This was NOT her usual path. At the sound of voices, she must have gone left instead of right. Now she had no idea where she was or how to get back to her small mouse hole that was just big enough for her to wiggle in, but not big enough for anything or anyone else to get in. She was lost.

Panic immediately set in and Lula wished her heart would beat 732 times a minute and cause her to faint so she would not have to deal with any of this, but it did not. For some unexplainable reason, her heart was calm and steady. She stood very still and looked around her. She had been gone so long that light was beginning to fill the hallway and she could hear more and more voices.

Lula noticed she was not far from a door that was open just a sliver and for once being little was a good thing. She could wiggle through. She was desperate to get out of this hallway as it became more and more crowded.

Still cautious she used every possible means to ensure her safety. Her ears may have been little, but they could hear the faintest sound. She had been told many times her eyes were small and beady, but she knew if she focused them in on something, she could see every detail.

Her mouse nose could sniff out even the faintest scent. She slowly crept down the hallway toward the door that was open just a sliver.

Her whole body - ears, eyes, nose - on high alert. Lula had never allowed herself to be in this position of not knowing exactly where she was or what she was doing EVER! Yet for some unknown reason she was still calm. The closer she got to the door the more she seemed to be drawn to go inside. What a strange new feeling.

Unlike the small opening to her mouse hole that only she could wiggle through, this door was bigger than any door she had ever seen. Lula scampered by doors every day that were bigger than her mouse hole, but they were simply made of wood and allowed humans to go in and out. This door was made of heavy wood with gold hinges. Every other door Lula had ever seen was plain, but this door had a carving of a gorgeous tree and beautiful flowers. Graceful birds were flying above the tree. But what caught Lula's full attention was all the animals beautifully carved into the face of the door. Some she recognized like the dogs and cats, but others she had no idea even existed or what they were called. Even beyond all that, what stuck in her mind was the carving of a mouse with a crown on its head. There simply was no explanation why a mouse would be carved on this grand door. A mouse with a crown was pure fantasy. Who or what could possibly be behind this door? For some strange reason she had to know.

CHAPTER 3

SAFE

BAM! Something had fallen. Lula was suddenly jolted back into real time. Her mind had wandered imagining what might be inside this door. She had left her safe place along the edge of the hallway and was standing in front of a huge unknown door that was opened only a sliver.

What was she thinking!!! She had almost forgotten about her need for a long-detailed plan to keep her safe, but now her mind was racing. How could she get back to her mouse hole? She had to try and retrace her steps. She scurried as fast as her little feet would take her back down the long hallway. She took several turns that led her to dead ends. It was as if she was in a giant maze, but she kept running. The light was getting brighter and brighter. After several attempts she finally came to a hallway that she recognized. She quickly dashed past familiar landmarks until at last she saw her mouse hole. She almost collapsed just a few feet from her hole. It took every bit of her strength, but she managed to one more time wiggle herself though her mouse hole into the safety of her home.

The next several days Lula continued to shake. She would be fine and then suddenly it was like she was experiencing an earthquake inside her tiny body. She could not sleep without nightmares that she had been seen and captured. Fear washed over her every time she thought of how close she came to never seeing her little mouse home again. Longtail, Cheddar, and Belle all came to visit. Even though they did not really think of her as a friend, they knew she was always a part of the crowd that surrounded them. They would stand outside her mouse hole and try to comfort her because it was too small for anyone but Lula to wiggle through. She was back home where she was safe. She was back home where she had her detailed plan. But the fear of being lost again gripped her and she could not leave her mouse home.

Long Tail would stay outside her hole and tell her all about his wild adventures. He loved telling his stories to anyone who would listen. Some of his tales would make Lula forget for a moment what she had experienced, and she would laugh out loud at Long Tail's great escapes. Because Lula was too afraid to leave her mouse hole, Cheddar would stop by every day with some new cheese discovery. He was happy to give her a private lecture. She was grateful for Cheddar's kindness. And then there was Belle. Beautiful Belle would just come and sit right outside Lula's small mouse hole. Belle never felt the need to try to help Lula get over her fear and be able to leave her mouse hole. Belle was just there sharing how wonderful her life was.

Days turned to weeks and Lula continued to stay in her small, dark but safe hole. But she never forgot the door.

.

CHAPTER 4

THE DOOR

There was something about that door that Lula could not forget. She tried to not think about it. She tried to distract her mind by writing a more detailed plan for leaving her mouse hole. But still, she would find herself remembering every detail of the door. However, after a while she began to have doubts there even was a door. If there was a door, she wondered if she had only imagined seeing a mouse wearing a crown in her panic-stricken state. She had spent way too much time sitting around thinking about a door that might not even exist. Finally, after several weeks of not leaving the safety of her mouse home, she was determined to resume her daily routine. It was wrong to continue to depend on Long Tail, Cheddar, and Belle to change their daily routines for her.

The next morning, she was up even earlier than usual. She had gone over her path at least a hundred times in her head. She knew she would take 364 steps to her first turn to the left. From there every detail of her path was memorized. She would never allow herself to be lost again. She quickly came to the hole along the edge of the hallway that took her inside the room where she would find crumbs the little humans had dropped. She quickly gathered up a few crumbs and scurried back to her hole and wiggled through to safety. Each day was a little easier, even though the fear of being lost had not left her, neither had the memory of the door.

Now there was a new voice in her head. A voice that had been getting stronger each day as she faced a little more of the fear of leaving her mouse hole. She even made herself go just a little further from the edge of the wall to get a bigger crumb. A few weeks later, she went just a little further down the hallway than usual. One day she even discovered a shorter route to the hole in the hallway that led to food. Just yesterday she had forced herself to leave five minutes later than what was on her plan. Now she heard these very faint words in her ear, "You can do it." The memory of the door was once again real, and she could see every detail. The door was like a giant magnet pulling her against her need to be safe. Still, she was not ready to just throw caution to the wind and go looking for a door that might not even exist.

CHAPTER 5

FRIENDLY ADVICE?

Her cautious side advised her to ask those who knew about this kind of thing. Long Tail was first on her list. Long Tail had been so many places and had bone chilling tales of narrow escapes. Lula was sure if there was a grand door Long Tail would know about it and could advise her on a plan back to the door. She invited Long Tail over in the middle of the afternoon on a beautiful summer day. Long Tail did his best work when it was dark, so Lula had to adjust to his schedule. The opening for her mouse hole was only big enough for her to wiggle through so Lula and Long Tail sat in the hallway next to her mouse hole. She began slowly to tell Long Tail the entire story of the day she had gotten lost and finished by telling him about the beautiful door. She described the door in great detail and ended in a whisper as she told Long Tail that she had seen a mouse carved into this door.

Long Tail's mouth dropped wide open. For the first time ever, Lula saw Long Tail's jagged teeth. His eyes were as big as plates. He began to quiver and spoke in a broken squeak. "You must never go back there!" Lula was shocked. Surely there was nothing that would cause fear in the heart of a great adventurer like Long Tail. Long Tail was obviously shaken and not wanting anyone to see his fear he quickly turned and scampered away. Lula was left confused. Why had Long Tail reacted so strangely? The fearful side of Lula immediately said, "Well that settles it. I will not be going back to the door."

From Long Tail's reaction she now knew for sure the door did exist. For him to react so strongly had to mean he had seen the door. She did not understand why Long Tail had reacted so strangely. Lula knew this was no ordinary door. The door was big and grand. Surely that door would have to lead into something beyond her wildest imagination. Not quite willing to give up all hope, she waited a few days and invited Cheddar over for a visit. He too did his best work in the dark and came by in the afternoon just like Long Tail.

Lula proceeded with a little more care this time. She talked casually with Cheddar as they sat in the hallway outside her mouse hole and thanked him for coming over. Lula made sure Cheddar knew how much she appreciated all the wonderful cheese he had brought her when she was unable to leave her mouse home. Of course, Lula never ate all the cheese that Cheddar would bring each day. She always saved a little just in case she might need it for a rainy day. A rainy day just meant for a day when she was too afraid to go out. But today she went to her cupboard and brought out the cheese she had tucked away just in case she might need it someday and served it to Cheddar. It felt as if another piece of fear fell off Lula. Lula and Cheddar sat in the middle of the day out in the hallway eating cheese. Again, she heard the same, "You can do it" she had heard before and this time it was just a wee bit louder.

After Cheddar leaned back against the hallway wall with his stomach puffed out like a large cheese ball, Lula began to slowly tell Cheddar the whole story of the fear filled day when she got lost and discovered the door. At the mention of a huge wooden door with beautiful carvings and a mouse, Cheddar froze in mid burp. Lula watched as terror crept over his face. It was like watching spilled milk spread across the floor after a little human knocked over a glass. Cheddar was speechless. He turned around and scampered back to his hole. This was odd. Cheddar was never speechless. Lula now knew Cheddar also had to know about the door.

Lula was more confused than ever. Why would the mention of a huge door with beautiful carvings - one being a mouse - not fill Cheddar's mind with thoughts of massive cheese wedges? Why did hundreds of cheese plates not float through Cheddar's mind like clouds on a spring day? Surely a mouse whose home had a huge door with beautiful carvings and gold hinges would have only the best cheese and lots of it.

This was turning into quite the puzzle. There was one last hope – Belle. Belle could see the goodness in everything. She could put glitter on the worst possible situation and turn it into a thing of beauty. Surely, she would have words of wisdom. Lula once again waited and planned out her meeting with Belle down to which dress she would wear, the time of day, and what she would serve.

Finally the day and hour arrived, and Belle came in all her beauty. Lula wore her best dress. Lula's best dress was a scrap of fabric that had been thrown away held together with a staple. Belle was dressed like a Queen. They settled down at a small table outside Lula's mouse hole and the sound of Belle's joyous chatter could be heard up and down the hallway. Belle shared with Lula the gossip of the mouse nest in full detail. Lula only had to speak an occasional word like "really" or "that is so exciting."

Lula was getting ready to bring out a small piece of cracker she had found and was saving for such a special occasion as this, but at that moment Belle opened the basket she had brought with her. She began setting out the prettiest tea set Lula had ever seen. Painted on the white plates were bright pink flowers. On each plate Belle placed a plump green grape. Lula had never eaten a grape. She had heard others talk about taking a bite and the juice running down their whiskers. Now it was Lula's turn to freeze. Not from fear but from the excitement of tasting for the first time something as prized as a grape.

Belle just went right on chattering and quickly nibbled away at the grape. Lula would take one nibble and then save the rest for later. Belle finally came to a pause in her chattering and Lula found the courage to speak. Courage was a brand-new feeling for Lula. Surely if anyone knew about things like a huge, beautiful door that had the feeling of royalty, it would have to be Belle.

Lula began to tell Belle her story of the day she got lost and discovered a door of such beauty that she had not forgotten it to this day. Lula began to talk faster as she told of the carvings of a tree and flowers and all the animals. With each word her excitement grew like a balloon being pumped full of air. Then she told Belle what she had not even mentioned to Long Tail and Cheddar. She told Belle that on this huge, beautiful door there was a carving of a mouse with a crown on his head. Just as the words mouse and crown came out of Lula's mouth, Belle dropped her teacup and her entire expression changed from one of beauty to one of anger as she spoke these words to Lula. "Such things as these are not for little mice like you." With that she picked up her things and left.

CHAPTER 6

NOT FOR LITTLE MICE LIKE YOU

The words, "such things as these are not for little mice like you" bounced back and forth in Lula's head like a ping pong ball being batted back and forth over a net. The words jerked her back with a force that was quick and painful. Who did Lula think she was? Of course, this magnificent door with the beautiful carvings of a tree, flowers, animals, and a mouse with a crown would never be opened for a little mouse like her. An invitation into that room would be reserved for someone like beautiful Belle.

Every time Lula thought of the reactions of Long Tail, Cheddar, and Belle her little mouse body went go limp. They must know something about the door that she did not. If they did not think it was safe for them to go to the door, then it certainly was not safe for her. She quickly went back to being just little Lula that no one saw. She went back to her orderly routine of getting up early and hugging close to the edge of the hallway until she came to the hole that opened into a room where she could always find food. She would enter silently, gather a few crumbs, and then leave unseen and unnoticed arriving back at her mouse home without any unexpected or surprising events.

Summer finally gave way to fall and a cold chill began to settle into mouse homes everywhere. This time of the year space had to be made for their country cousins who lived out in the fields in the summer. When the air became crisp, they would need to stay with their cousins inside through the winter. That meant there were a lot more mouths to feed and food would become scarce. Most mice families would have friends and family that would stay the winter with them, but no one stayed with Lula. Even though it was crowded and food was scarce, the sound of mouse squeals could be heard all through the night and the patter of little mice feet on the hallway floor. They scampered from hole to hole catching up with all the mouse cousins. All winter Lula would wiggle through her tiny opening into her tiny home and listen to the squeaks and squeals as families enjoyed time together. Despite trying to erase the memory of the door from her mind, her mind would wander back down the hallway along the edge of the floor to the door. She would once again be overcome by a feeling deep inside her that she was meant to go through that door.

Just when Lula thought those long and lonely nights would never end, word began to echo down the hallways and into all the mice holes that spring had arrived. Goodbyes could be heard in every direction as the field mice once again left to go back outside. There was a different feel in the air. It seemed like all of nature was breaking out in new colors, new growth, and new excitement. Lula felt it in her bones. She had lived a somewhat happy life but there had to be more. She had to know what was behind the huge wooden door carved with a tree and flowers. She had to find out about the beautiful carvings of animals and the mouse with a crown.

Lula sat down and made a plan. She had a fairly good idea of where the door was, but she had to be certain. Each day she would begin her search for the door. She kept a detailed drawing with exactly how many steps she took and which way she turned. Time after time she would end up at a dead end and need to retrace her steps back to her mouse hole. But slowly and surely, she got further each day. Then on a spring day in May she took step 487, rounded the corner and there was the door – her door. Her heart stopped, fear gripped her until she could hardly breath and she raced home faster than her little legs had ever gone before. Once safe in her mouse home she flung herself into her chair and breathed a long deep breath. She was home safe, and she now knew how to find the door.

Lula had the exact map to the door. She could go anytime she wanted and not be afraid of getting lost. Lula felt more alive than she could ever remember. For the

next several days she followed her map to the exact point where she took step 487, turned the corner, and there was the door. It took weeks to finally take step 488.

The Secret Behind The Door

CHAPTER 7

BRAVERY

Then one day she took step 488. There was not anything special about that day. Lula did not even make a detailed plan for the day she just took step 488. It just happened. She took step 488 which immediately led to step 489. She found herself standing right at the tiny sliver at the side of the door she had first discovered months ago.

The door was exactly like she had remembered and more. Yes, there was a mouse with a crown carved into the door. The mouse was bigger and grander than she had even remembered. She stood in front of the door several minutes just looking up at its beauty. Surely this door led to something beyond her wildest imagination. Then Lula did the unthinkable. She wiggled her little body through the sliver at the side of the door and she entered the room.

Even though Lula had gone way beyond anything she had ever done before, she still wanted to be safe. She

headed to the edge of the room and snuggled as close to the wall as she could get. She stayed perfectly still hardly daring to even breathe. She calmed her heart beat down well below the maximum rate of 632 beats per minute. Very slowly she began to look around. Her ears were on high alert, her beady little eyes laser focused on every detail of the room, and her nose was going crazy as she was sniffing smells that were strange and new.

The huge door now seemed tiny in comparison to the magnificent room it revealed. The beauty of the carvings on the door were just a sampling of what she now saw. Even in her wildest dreams she could never have imagined something this grand. It was so beautiful she now feared she would faint but was shocked that her heart was not wildly beating beyond the maximum rate of 632 times per minute. Strangely she felt her heart slow down. Then Belle's words exploded in her mind, "Such things as these are not for little mice like you." Those words were like a stab in her heart. She took comfort in the thought that if she never came back, she had at least been here once.

And then she ran. She ran straight across the middle of the floor her little feet scampering faster than a runaway train. Her beady little eyes were like lasers focused on the sliver at the side of the huge door that would allow her to go to her home. Her safe place.

What happened next Lula was never quite sure

about but suddenly she hit what felt like a brick wall head on. She felt herself being hoisted into the air by her tiny tail and she was swaying back and forth. Of all the horrors she had heard from Long Tail, Cheddar, and even Belle about things to avoid at all cost, swaying by your tail had never been mentioned. She knew to avoid what looked like easy cheese that was on a piece of wood because it was connected to a bar that could swiftly come down and trap you. She knew she must never try to eat from any type of unfamiliar container. Many a mouse had been tricked to think colorful little pellets were easy pickings but would later realize that the pellets were not food. But never in her entire life had Lula heard a story of a mouse hanging by their tail.

She waited and then her fear grew to extreme terror as she realized she was being held by a guard who had been standing in front of the door. How had she missed him? She had been so focused on the sliver at the edge of the door that she had missed the gigantic guard standing right in front of the door. He was now looking at Lula with surprise in his eyes. Lula then felt herself being carried across the room and placed down on top of a tall pillar of stone. There was no escape. She was so high up that if she tried to jump down, she would be hurt. The stone was so smooth she could not possibly climb down the side. She made herself as small as possible hoping she was now invisible.

Then it happened. The moment that would change

Lula forever. Out of the vastness of this room she heard a voice. A voice that was strong and powerful, yet somehow gentle and kind. The words she heard spoken were written on Lula's heart that day and no matter what she faced the rest of her life she would never forget them.

"Welcome Lula I love you and I have been waiting for you."

With those words ringing in her ears, she dared to look up. Then she saw Him. Her mind flashed back to the mouse on the door. She could not believe she had missed it. This was no ordinary mouse that was carved into the huge door. It was a King. Her mind had not been able to believe a mouse could be a King. She was now looking into the loving eyes of the King carved on the door wearing a crown. His eyes sparkled like diamonds in the sunlight. It was as if the darkness she had hidden in all her life was gone and now there was light all around. For some unknown reason, she was not afraid to be in the light. She was not afraid to be seen by the King who wore a crown.

The Secret Behind The Door

CHAPTER 8

THE KING

Time seemed to stand still. In the presence of the King, everything was calm, peaceful, and filled with light. Lula was shocked when the King told her he knew her when she was just a pinkie (baby mouse). He told her exactly where she lived and knew that her mouse hole was so small only she could wiggle through. The King laughed that she was up earlier than anyone else to go find food before the light began to shine in through the windows. He said He loved early risers. The King knew that she never ventured into the middle of any room even if she saw a big piece of cheese. Lula could not believe this King knew everything about her and He still loved her.

The thought that someone else knew so much about her would normally have caused her to shrink even smaller, but this was different. The thought of the King knowing her, watching over her, and loving her filled her with such a sense of amazement that she thought for a moment she might float in the air like a balloon filled with helium. His next words were unbelievable. He – the King - told her she was His daughter. Then He said that everything He had was hers. She bit her tail! Twice!! This was a dream and she needed to wake up immediately. Instead of waking up, she heard herself shriek "OUCH." She looked up and saw the King's eyes sparkling like the lights she would see at Christmas time. The King was smiling at her and this was not a dream.

This was all little Lula could take in for one day. The King told the guard to lift her down off the pillar and make sure she got safely back to her home. Lula was escorted like a Queen down the hallway. The guard stayed and watched to make sure she had wiggled through her tiny little hole before he left.

Once inside Lula leapt into her chair. (Just so you know mice can leap nearly 18 inches) On this day Lula leapt from her doorway to her chair which was at least 20 inches. Then she did the unthinkable. Lula turned on her lamp for no reason. The lamp in Lula's home was never turned on accept when she was working on a long-detailed plan. The rest of the time it was there only for decoration. Something had changed in Lula and now she wanted her home to be filled with light all the time. All her life she thought the darkness hid her and kept her safe. Now she craved the light. The light reminded her of the King and that He loved her. When she was in the King's light, she was truly safe.

Lula tossed and turned all night long in her bed. When she finally woke, she had overslept and missed her opportunity to go out before others were in the hallway. Lula was so busy going over everything that had happened the day before she did not even think about food.

Lula went straight back to her chair where the lamp was still on. She picked up the book where she kept all her important information and began to write down the events of the day before. She recorded going to the door, wiggling through the sliver at the side, running across the middle of the floor, being swung in the air by her tail and placed on a huge pillar. All of that was important, but it was the words that the King had spoken to her that she never wanted to forget.

"Welcome Lula I love you and I have been waiting for you."

He knew everything about her. He said she was His daughter. The King said she lived in His castle and all that was His was hers. A guard had escorted to her home like a Queen. She would hide all this in her heart and not share her discovery with Long Tail, Cheddar, or Belle. At least not yet.

The Secret Behind The Door

CHAPTER 9

DANGER

Every day Lula made her way back to the door that led to the King. Her guardian was always there to lift her up on the pillar so she and the King could talk. She never worried about food now. The King would always have plenty. Every day Lula was learning more and more about the King and the rules of His Kingdom to keep her safe. When Lula and the King had finished talking, her guardian would escort her through the hallways like a Queen.

Lula wished she had found the King when she was just little. She thought about all the years she had spent in the dark. Getting up early every morning and scurrying down a dark hallway to the same hole to hide along the edge of the same wall. She thought about all the times she had gathered crumbs when she could have been feasting with the King. It was almost more than she could bear. But now she was determined to make up for lost time and not miss another minute of enjoying her new life with the King.

Even though the King's castle was a place of beauty and filled with light, her guardian quickly made her aware that there were dangers even in the castle for her to avoid. Lula was to always call for the King when she needed help. She was to study the King's rules so she would know what she should avoid. Lula was sure she would never do anything foolish.

The castle quickly became her new home. There were so many rooms to discover. The words of the King that He loved her had changed everything. She now found that anytime fear and darkness came her way, she could call out to the King and His light would always scatter fear and darkness.

One day as Lula was out and about enjoying everything about the new world of the King's castle, she saw another door. Just like the King's door it was beautiful, and it was open just a sliver at the side. Lula thought hard. Was this a door that the King had told her not to go in and that her guardian had warned her about? She really could not quite remember. These days Lula was not the same fear- filled mouse she had once been. Day by day, as she sat and talked with the King and ate from His table, she had grown strong and bold. She looked about for her guardian, but he did not seem to be around and instead of searching for him or calling for the King, she decided she could do some exploring on her own.

Just like the King's door this door seemed to be like a magnet pulling her inside. But there was just something that felt different in Lula's heart. When she got closer, she could hear music and laughter inside the door. Surely this was something good the King had not yet told her about. She felt a strong tug in her heart now. It was as if she was being pulled away from this door, but she ignored it and wiggled her body through the sliver at the side of this door and then BAM! That same BAM she had heard when she first stood before the King's door yet quite different. This time the BAM was not something falling, but the door slamming shut behind her.

Now the room where she had heard music and laughter was filled with darkness. Lula immediately knew this was one of the dangers the King had warned her about. This room could be filled with dangerous traps. She knew she should immediately let out the loudest squeal she could squeal, but she did not want the King to know she had disobeyed. Lula did not want the King to be disappointed in her. What if He was mad at her and told her to leave the castle?

Instead of squealing for help, Lula made the choice to handle this herself. In the darkness she could not even see where the door was. It was as if it had vanished and there was no way out. She began to move cautiously around the edge of the room like she did before she met the King. Then SNAP and instant pain. She felt a deep throbbing pain in her little back foot. She began to struggle but she could not break free.

At that moment, her fear of being trapped in this dark place was greater than her fear of telling the King who loved her that she had disobeyed. She let out a squeal that could be heard in every corner of the castle. Immediately the King dispatched Lula's guardian to rescue her. The guardian carried the light of the King's presence with him and the darkness scattered. The guardian quickly released Lula's little back foot from the trap and carried her to the King.

When the King saw Lula, His eyes were not filled with anger. What Lula saw in the King's face was love and concern for her. The King took her into His arms and the throbbing pain her foot was gone. As the King continued to hold her, He showed her that one of the five toes on her back foot was missing.

The King explained to her that the rules and boundaries He set for her were never meant to keep her from joy and happiness. Just the opposite. The rules and boundaries were set because the King had enemies who were always trying to trick His children into disobeying. After telling Lula she was forgiven for disobeying, her guardian escorted her like a Queen through the hallways as she hobbled home to rest.

A long time ago, Lula had widened the opening to her home and now friends and family were always coming in and out. She always had her lamp turned on, so her

home was bright and cheery. After the toe incident, Lula was the talk of the mouse nest. As others came by, they would tell her stories they had heard about how she lost a toe. At some of the stories Lula would just shake her head but others sent her into hysterical laughter. According to one story, Lula got so tired of her family and friends getting caught in mouse traps she decided to take action. She snuck out of the castle and went to the mouse trap factory determined to stop the machines that made mouse traps. She was gnawing through the electrical wires that ran the machines when suddenly she felt electricity causing her whiskers to curl. She jumped back and landed on a mouse trap. Still buzzing with electricity, she leapt two feet into the air leaving her little toe behind. Lula laughed so hard she fell out of her chair. That was certainly not how it happened, but it was funny. Lula always made sure that everyone who came to her heard the truth of how she disobeyed the King and that He forgave her and still loved her.

Her heart was sad that Long Tail, Cheddar, and Belle could never believe that she had found the King and that she was His daughter. Even though they could see with their own eyes that Lula had changed, they would not go with her to meet the King. But many others did. When Lula had lost her toe, she thought that it would be a constant reminder of her disobedience (and it did keep her from ever going through that door of darkness again) but somehow the King had allowed her to use her story to invite others to meet Him and many did.

The Secret Behind The Door

CHAPTER 10

THE DUNGEON

Lula's life settled into a wonderful routine of daily meeting with the King. The King even asked her to begin teaching others the basic rules of the His castle. She left her home and moved into the room where she first wiggled through the door that opened her life to the King. Lula no longer kept back crumbs in case she could not find food. In her Father's house there was always an abundance. Now she could hardly remember the little fear-filled mouse she once was. She had grown in her love and obedience to the King. Every day was spent serving Him.

Then life changed again. It was just an ordinary Thursday. Still an early riser, Lula was with the King one morning when their conversation took a strange turn. He began to tell Lula about the dungeon beneath the castle. Of course, Lula had heard stories about the dungeon. Only the bravest and most fierce warriors were called to go down into the belly of the castle to rescue those who were trapped.

Lula had no idea why the King would be talking to her about the dungeon. The King went on to tell Lula how proud He was of how she had grown from the little fear-filled mouse He first met into the faithful servant she had become. He had watched her change from being afraid to allow anyone into her life to joyfully widening her mouse hole so friends and family could constantly come and go anytime of the night or day. Many had reported to Him of how her teachings were helping them to change. Then he told her something about herself she never knew. The King told her that the name He had chosen for her from the time she was a pinkie (baby mouse) was Lula AND that her name meant "Fierce Warrior".

Lula could not contain herself and began to laugh at the thought of being a fierce warrior. Remember even for a mouse she was little. Fierce! She was the opposite of fierce and that would be gentle. Warrior! She had seen warriors come back from the belly of the dungeon with their armor on and their swords at their side. Swords just gave her the creeps.

The king's gaze never left her. He was looking directly into her eyes just like the day He said to her "Welcome Lula I love you and I have been waiting for you." Now He was saying "Lula I have called you to be a fierce warrior for me and help rescue others."

Her thoughts were swirling like the winds around

a tornado with the words fierce, warrior, go, and dungeon! Just moments before Lula had been happy and comfortable. But now Lula felt like everything was about to change and she was not sure she liked the feeling. The truth was she liked her life here with the King. She liked always being close to Him and talking to others about Him. She was content and most of all she felt safe.

The King continued to gaze into Lula's eyes as He said the choice was hers. He would always love her no matter what she chose. But to grow in His love, she had to be willing to conquer even more of her fear and risk danger to rescue others. Lula knew in her heart of hearts that she would say yes. He was her King and had not kept back anything from her. She would not keep back anything in her life from Him. But she still said, "I will think about it." Think on it she did. Day and Night. Night and Day. She came up with a "for" and "against" list. She had come up with 159 reasons against accepting this assignment. The only reason for accepting the assignment was one word, "Obey." After 10 days, 14 hours, and 36 minutes from the ordinary Thursday the King asked her to go and rescue others Lula said, "Yes I will take your message of love to those who are in the dungeon." Another door was opening in Lula's life.

Lula was still a planner. She set down and made her lists. She found out who had been to the dungeon and asked them every question she could think of and made sure to record every answer in her notebook. She gathered up the armor that the fierce warriors told her she would need in the dungeon. She would need a belt of truth, a shield of faith, a helmet, and SHOES. New fiery red shoes were on the top of her list. Then she took sword fighting lessons. It took some practice to learn to swing her sword without knocking off her helmet. On another ordinary Thursday, the King called her and said to her, "I am sending you with my message of love to Todd who is now living in the dungeon."

Early the next morning Lula put on her armor and hung her sword on her side. She began to go down the long winding steps to the dungeon. The air was heavy with moisture and the dampness made the steps slippery. Lula could not stop a small smile from slowly crossing her face. Shoes were a vital part of her armor. Every fierce warrior had to make sure their footwear was sturdy and would keep them from slipping. Footwear meant new shoes! It was almost, but not quite, a reason for a trip to the dungeon. She had to search high and low on shelf after shelf to find the perfect pair. Remember Lula was a small little mouse which meant she had little feet and one foot had a toe missing. Finally, she saw them. The perfect pair of shoes in a gorgeous red and it was happy dance time in the shoe aisle. The guys were always happy to go to camouflage combat boot section but only a few danced. Now her steps were sure as she walked confidently deeper and deeper into the belly of the dungeon.

CHAPTER 11

LULA FINDS TODD

Lula had spent most of her life in dark places. Even though she now lived in the light of the King's presence, every day she would go back out into the dark places inside the castle with her story of the King's love. But the darkness in the dungeon was different. Slowly her beady little eyes adjusted. Her first discovery was that the dungeon was a wide-open space. There were NO walls. No locked doors. No chains to hold anyone in this dark place. Why were there so many here, who were they, and why did they not just leave were just a few of the questions running through her mind. It seemed everyone in the dungeon was very sad and lonely.

She continued to carefully explore this dark eerie place. She pulled the sides of her helmet snuggly around her head. The helmet protected her mind from any thoughts that were not from the King. She would need to stay focused and not allow her mind to wander off as it often did.

There were so many thoughts to think about but that would have to wait. Right now, she was hunting for the one the King had sent her to find. Where in this eerie dungeon was Todd? There were so many mice and without any signs there was nothing to show the name of each mouse. She finally decided to just begin asking each mouse if they were Todd and if they said no, she would ask if they knew Todd.

She asked mouse after mouse with the same result. No, they were not Todd and they did not know Todd. Just when she was beginning to feel confident that she could handle the assignment the King had given her; she turned the corner and turned white as a sheet. Around the corner there were no mice. It was filled with CATS!

All her life she had lived in absolute fear of cats. Long Tail, Cheddar, and Belle all had told tales that made Lula's her ears burn. Now she was face to face with cat after cat. All different sizes and colors. Then a memory from long ago floated back into her mind. The first time she had laid eyes on the door she remembered that there were animals she had never seen before and had no idea what their names were. Lula also remembered there were dogs and CATS. Cats were carved into the King's door so He must love cats. How could the King love cats? Lula thought of cats as her enemy.

As she stood there it felt as if fiery darts were piercing her heart. She began to doubt that the King was as good and loving as He had said. She began to doubt that He would protect her here in this place of such sadness, loneliness, and now cats. Suddenly her guardian was beside her telling her to pick up the shield of faith she had dropped at the sight of the cats and hold it over her heart. The moment she did the bad thoughts would hit the shield and simply bounce off. She fixed her thoughts on what she knew to be true. The King had always loved her and protected her. The King had never lied to her. She had heard many times, and had taught it to others, that the King loved everyone. It now exploded in her mind that included cats. So onward she went asking each cat if their name was Todd.

On and on she went in search of the one named Todd. Some of the animals she saw she had heard about from the field mice but some of the animals were simply weird looking. She kept asking each animal why they did not just leave because there were no doors, no locks, and no chains. No one could explain this strangeness, but they all spoke of feeling like a heavy blanket of sadness and loneliness was weighing them down. They said their fear felt like chains around their ankles that would not let them leave. Lula knew these words were not used by the King.

Lula's heart was broken for all the animals. Her heart broke for the animals she knew and those she did not know and yes, even the cats. She could certainly understand why the King would send fierce warriors to this place with His light and message of freedom and joy. It made Lula smile that when others saw just a small mouse the King saw a fierce warrior.

She began to think that if there had once been a Todd in this place, that was no longer true. Lula would ask one more animal. This time a pig. Yes, a pig. Lula was quite proud of herself for knowing the pig from a detailed description she once heard while sitting on a dark winter night in the family nest listening to one of the field mice. She remembered the description of the pig's nose. It was described like two round tubes the mice would find on the floor after all the paper had been used from them. The hole on the end of the tube was used for breathing. She was also told that the pigs used their noses to dig in the mud and dirt. How could you breathe with your nose filled with yucky mud and dirt? Lula almost giggled now at the thought of trying to breathe through a nose clogged with smelly mud but managed to catch the giggle just before it came out. But the sure sign it was a pig was the tail. Short and curled. She thought her tail was short but compared to her body her tail was long. Now the pig had a large plump body with an itty-bitty tail. His tail compared to the size of his body was truly short and oddly curled. How could a short curly tail be of benefit to any animal? Lula had no idea and no time to ask. She asked the question she had been asking all day, "Is your name Todd?" That was all the further she got. Out of this pig came a squeal that made the squeal Lula had made when she bit her tail twice sound like a whisper. Fear made the pig's entire large body tremble. Yes he knew Todd, but no one ever even thought about going near Todd.

Boosted by the knowledge that she finally knew where Todd was and that the King was calling her to love all animals, Lula continued to walk. Corners! Why must there always be a corner just before something surprising. Why couldn't Lula ever see what was coming from a long way off and make a long-detailed plan? What she saw when she turned that corner was unbelievable. It was as if wet cement had been poured over her head and hardened. She was unable to move. What she saw was a fire breathing DRAGON! How did she know anything about fire breathing dragons you ask? Lula had once found a crumpled-up piece of paper dropped by a little human that she had gleefully taken back to her mouse hole to use as soft lining in her nest. As she began to rip it into tiny shreds, she caught sight of a creature that stirred her interest. She had carefully unfolded the paper and there was a picture of the most frightful animal anyone could ever imagine. It was an animal that would appear only in nightmares. She had quickly shredded the paper into the tiniest bits imaginable so that she would never be reminded of this frightening creature again. And now she was standing face to face with her nightmare. This could not be Todd! The King would never ask her to do something this dangerous. Lula's heart was pounding like a jack hammer that broke away the cement and she ran.

CHAPTER 12

THE BEGINNING OF A FRIENDSHIP

Lula turned and ran past the pig. She ran past animals that she knew and animals she did not know. Lula ran past the cats (which now seemed tame in comparison to a fire breathing dragon) and past the mice. Back up the slippery stairs with no thought of being careful and watching her step. On she ran down the hallway past the mouse hole where she once lived. Now she was running full speed down the hallway to the King's door. BAM!!! When would she remember there was always a guard at the King's door?

When Lula woke up, she was being held by her guardian. Her guardian gently placed her in the King's arms. Lula was once again overwhelmed by the love of the King for her. She still had so much to learn and so much growing up to do. But for this moment she was safe and loved by the King.

Lula rested in the arms of the King until dinner

time. The King's table was always filled with delicious fancy foods. Another chunk of fear broke off Lula remembering that with the King she had everything she needed. After she had eaten and her strength had returned, the King began to ask her about her trip to the dungeon. She told Him all about her discoveries. She told Him about the cats and how she was still thinking about loving cats. They laughed together as she told the story of the pig with the curly tail. Then Lula was silent. The King then asked her if she had discovered anyone after the pig (of course He already knew but wanted Lula not to keep any secrets from Him). Lula barely whispered – "I found Todd."

She began to describe Todd to the King. Todd was in an area all alone. Even though there were no walls or doors, Todd seemed to be held there by chains of fear and the heaviness of sadness and loneliness. But in Lula's eyes Todd was still a fire breathing dragon. The King would remind her that what she saw on the outside was not the real Todd. The King reminded Lula of how others had once seen her. When others saw Lula, they saw a small ordinary mouse always hiding in the background. The King reminded Lula of how He had always seen her – a Fierce Warrior! The King saw Todd very differently from how others saw Todd and so should she.

Early the next morning Lula left the King's presence and made her way back down the hallway. Back past the mouse hole that had once been her home and down the slippery stairs. Once again past the mice, the cats, and animals she knew and animals she did not know. Lula was giggling as she went past the pig. Then there was Todd. For a long time, Lula just stood and stared at Todd trying to imagine what wondrous thing the King saw in Todd the fire breathing dragon. Everything that Lula was not – Todd was. When she first met the King, Lula was even smaller than most mice. Todd was the largest animal Lula had ever seen. No one was afraid of Lula; Todd was feared by all the other animals. Lula had seemed invisible. You could not hide Todd. No one was ever concerned whether Lula was anywhere around, but Todd breathed fire for heaven's sake! Everyone was always worried about the whereabouts of Todd.

It was as if Todd suddenly felt someone close by and slowly turned and stared into the beady little eyes of Lula. Surprisingly, Lula stared deep into the eyes of Todd. For a moment both were trying to figure out what the other one was doing there. Todd could not believe that a tiny little mouse had dared to come near, and Lula was stunned at why someone as awesome as Todd would be in the dungeon. At that moment, an odd friendship began.

It took a few days, but Lula and Todd finally felt safe with one another and began to share their stories. Lula told Todd of all the things that had been said to her to make her feel little and worthless. One time an important mouse had told her the name Lula was not good enough and she needed to change her name. He said Lula was a funny sounding name. She should have a name that would command the attention of those in high places. Another time Lula was in a group listening to someone talking about his plans for the future. He wanted to have more money and toys than anyone else. When Lula shared her plan to live a simple happy life and be kind to others everyone laughed and told Lula she needed a bigger plan than that. Everywhere she went the Long Tails, Cheddars, and Belles were in the limelight and Lula was always in the shadows. Lula remained unseen, unnoticed, and never expected to accomplish anything great. Then one day she somehow found the courage to enter the King's door and her whole life changed forever.

When Lula finished that sentence, Todd began to share his story. Every time someone saw Todd, the fire breathing dragon, they EXPECTED something great. Todd was always the center of attention. Everyone expected wise answers when they were talking with the great fire breathing dragon. Other times if Todd just showed up everyone would run in fear just because dragons are enormous and have scales. Even though the dungeon had no doors or locks, Todd felt there was no way to ever change the way a fire breathing dragon would be seen by others and so he stayed.

Lula slowly began to tell Todd how her relationship with the King had changed her from little Lula to a Fierce Warrior. The fact that Lula was standing there in the

Lula began to see Todd with the eyes of the King. She saw the kindest heart she had ever seen. He always tried to show kindness to any animal who needed help. Todd was a defender. Anytime Todd would hear of a larger animal bullying someone smaller, he would show up and the mean behavior stopped. Lula discovered that Todd was a great listener. Every time Todd's mouth would begin to open everyone would hide expecting fire to spew out and burn everything in its path. Even though that was not true, Todd learned that when he was around others it was better to keep his mouth shut. Todd's mouth was shut most of the time. Lula knew that was another thing she could learn from Todd. Even though she could not breathe fire, her mouth seemed to be open all the time and often got her into trouble. Sometimes she would be wise to keep her mouth shut. Todd was so gentle, but sadly everyone could not see past the obvious outward appearance of a fire breathing dragon.

Todd was truly amazing. Now how could she help Todd accept the fact that the King did not see from the outside in but from the inside out. Todd had to meet the King. Bravery is a long slow process even for a fire breathing dragon. But one day Todd decided enough was enough and he was tired of feeling sad and lonely all the time. Lula's story kept playing in his head like a catchy song. Todd wanted what Lula had found and had decided to leave the dungeon and find the King.

Todd was not quick to decide, but once the decision was made look out. Lula and Todd were on their way out of the dungeon. You would think it would be easy for a fire breathing dragon to leave anywhere anytime they wanted. You would be wrong! The moment word spread throughout the dungeon that Todd was on the move, fear filled the dungeon like a siren going off in the middle of the night causing everyone to run for cover.

Groups of animals built huge walls to keep Todd from passing through their area. When others saw the walls, fear filled them like a fire hose filling a small glass. It seemed like there was a plot to keep Todd from getting out of the dungeon. Lula knew that fear was spreading through the dungeon and fear was never from the King. She also knew that the King's love was greater than fear.

It was time for Lula to live up to her name. This was the time and place for her to be the fierce warrior that the King had called her to be. She would not allow fear to hold her and Todd back. Her hand slid slowly down her side and took hold of the top of her sword. This was no ordinary sword. This sword would release the power of the King's words. When the sword was in the hand of someone who loved the King, the sword was a powerful weapon that could stop anything, even fear. Today Todd would be set free from the dungeon and welcomed into the King's Kingdom.

Lula accepted her assignment to rescue Todd from

the dungeon knowing the King would be with her. Lula bravely led Todd past everything that was placed in their way. There was nothing that could stop Lula and Todd from breaking through the chains of fear and leaving the heavy blanket of sadness and loneliness behind.

With every step Lula felt the power of the King leading her and Todd the fire breathing dragon out of the dark and eerie dungeon. Todd felt lighter with every step. All the loneliness and sadness began to break off like icicles falling off the roof on a warm day. Together a mouse and a fire breathing dragon were unstoppable when they trusted the King.

Lula no longer needed a map or a detailed plan to find the King. She knew the way and led Todd to the door she had wiggled through so long ago that had brought her into the King's presence. Now she boldly entered the room and led Todd to the King. The King spoke these words –

"Welcome Todd, I love you and I have been waiting for you."

Lula thought her heart would burst with joy when she heard the King welcome Todd. But then the King looked right at Lula and told her to come and stand with Todd in front of Him. Her heart was pounding so fast she could not begin to count how far over the 632 beats a minute that were normal for a mouse. But she knew she was over 632. Then her King spoke to her, "Lula you have fully accepted your name Lula on this day. You are truly a fierce warrior willing to face all fear to rescue others. However, Lula is not your full name. Your full name is Libelula which means Dragonfly. This day you will continue to rescue others as you take the sword you have been given, but today I give you wings of love. You have learned that there is nothing that can stop My love."

Then the King turned toward Todd and said, "Todd I think you are amazing. I would not change a thing. Everything about you is perfect even your size and your ability to breathe fire. You were created with a special purpose for your life. Your name means clever and smart and I want you to never hide who I created you to be."

"You will protect and defend those who are all alone with no one to watch over them. Your kind heart will draw you to those who are weak and hurting. I see your gentleness guided by your fierce love for those who are weak and need help. You will protect, defend, and guard many and nothing will stop you. Just like you once were, there are many who are held by fear and feel like they are weighed down by a heavy blanket of sadness and loneliness. I will send you to rescue them. You were created to do great things in my Kingdom."

And with those words, Liebelula flew on her new wings of love and sat on top of Todd's head. Lula and Todd would remain Best Friends Forever. Together the King would send them on many adventures into dark and dangerous places to bring the message of the King's love. In their wildest imaginations Lula and Todd could have never dreamed of what the King had planned for them.

The Secret Behind The Door

THE KING LOVES YOU TOO!

"Welcome _____ I love you and
I have been waiting for you."

I have chosen you to be my child.
When you accept my invitation, you will live in my
Kingdom of love. I cannot wait to spend time with you
every day. We will talk about anything that makes you
sad and share with each other what makes us laugh. If
you need anything you can come to me and ask. I will
never leave you alone. I have great plans for your life.
You never need to be afraid. Just call out to me for help
and I am with you. Together we will face everything that
concerns you.

Remember I am not looking on the outside. I am
looking at your beautiful heart. I saw you before you were
born and beamed with pride. I saw you on your birthday
and I danced and sang with joy.

So today _____Date_____we
set out on a great adventure. Yes, some days may be scary,
but I am with you. Yes, some days may be confusing to you
but remember I have a detailed plan for each day of your
life. Trust me. Together we will fill each day to the brim
with love and then let it overflow to everyone we meet.

Your life is the most valuable gift I have given you.
Because of the abundance you find in My Kingdom, every
day will be like Christmas as you go about giving out
gifts of love, joy, peace, patience, kindness, goodness,
faithfulness, gentleness, and self-control to everyone you
meet.

Your loving Father,

King Jesus

Made in the USA
Monee, IL
21 May 2022